Fires of Damnation

Hayley Briana

Copyright © 2024 by Hayley Briana

All rights reserved. No part of this publication may be reproduced, stored or transmitted in any form or by any means, electronic, mechanical, photocopying, recording, scanning, or otherwise, without written permission from the publisher. It is illegal to copy this book, post it to a website, or distribute it by any other means without permission.

<u>DON'T BE A DICK WHO STEALS FROM AUTHORS!</u>

This novel is entirely a work of fiction. The names, characters, and incidents portrayed in it are the work of the author's imagination. Any resemblance to actual persons, living or dead, events or localities is entirely coincidental.

Hayley Briana asserts the moral right to be identified as the author of this work.

First Edition

ISBN: 979-8-9874871-9-8

ASIN: B0CLQRCCGR

For those whose drug of choice is a pretty boy with tattoos and a dark side. You know, because he just looks like he could fuck you good and dirty.

NOTE TO THE READER

This book contains explicit content and dark themes that may be traumatic and offensive to some readers. It is intended only for those 18 years or older.

For a full list of triggers, please visit the author's website HayleyBrianaWrites.com

***

<u>Scan with your phone camera to see a full list of triggers</u>

Playlist

"Sand" - Dove Cameron

"Bad Things" - Nation Haven

"Deep Dive" - Zaryah

"When You Say My Name" - Chandler Leighton

"Like a Drug" - Bryce Savage

"Fire & Smoke" - BEECH LOVE

"Bite Marks" - Ari Abdul

"Cravin'" - Stileto, Kendyle Paige

Prologue

Another long night at the club had my feet aching in these tall as shit shoes. It was a wonder I didn't twist an ankle while dancing tonight.

"Fucking, Rodney." I mumbled under my breath, lighting a cigarette and taking a long drag.

The air was hot and humid tonight. One of those hot summer nights where the moon couldn't even chase away the heat of the sun. If I ever managed to get out of Georgia, I'd go somewhere that had cooler times of year.

This shit was for the birds.

Rodney had been a pain in my ass tonight. Pissed off that I'd put my two weeks in and that he couldn't convince me to stay. He even went as far as saying that when Rose turned eighteen in a few months, he'd snatch her up to dance for him, too.

Like hell if I would ever let that sleazebag get his hands on my little sister. Over my dead fucking body.

I finally had enough saved up to start a new life for me and my sister.

To hell with this place.

Stuffing my lighter and pack into my little strappy bag, I made my way down the sidewalk. Heading back to my last night in that shit ass apartment in the downtown area.

Tomorrow I would stuff everything we owned into that little damned car and I'd be happy to watch the sunrise through my rearview mirror. I'd drive as far west as we could get. Only stopping once a place seemed right.

I'd buy us a little plot of land out there with a cabin. One where we could get ourselves a stable of horses and other livestock. Grow our own food in a small field and live how mama had always dreamed we could.

She'd always wanted a farm. A little place to call home where no one could ever bother us.

A pang of sadness laced my heart every time I thought of mama in her last moments. The nurse coming in to check her vitals as she struggled to breathe. The cancer was already eating away at her final seconds.

Taking another drag of my cigarette, I watched as an old black car was heading this way. Not paying it much mind as I leaned against a light pole and bent to take off these damn shoes. Tetanus would be better than the blisters these bitches would cause. Them and all their siblings were going in the trash first thing tomorrow morning.

I'd never have to shake my ass for a buck again.

The next thing I knew the same black car was stopping next to me and strong arms wrapped around me from the alley at my back.

A scream tore through me as I fought to get free as hands pulled me into the car. Feeling a prick at my neck until everything went black.

Chapter One

Zack

This place was a fucked cesspool. Filled with rich assholes who got off on watching sex slaves drugged up and forced to do whatever they were told.

From the glassy looks in all their eyes, it was clear whoever they actually were as people was buried deep. I remember that feeling all too well, but my situation was so much different.

I chose that life. These people didn't.

It was hard to look at the debauchery of the place. It always had been to come to these things. This job never got easier, no matter how many times you were forced to take it all in.

I tried not to focus on the others in the room for long. Instead, I searched the room for Cherry. A sigh of relief leaving me when it was clear she wasn't on display tonight.

I watched as people found men dressed in all black suits and tablets in their hands. All of them placing bids as if they were at an auction to either have a night with one of the *entertainers* or outright purchase them for their own *private collections*.

It always baffled me how they could pull off such large-scale events. That these people were trafficked and brought here against their will. Every single one of the sick fucks in this room getting off on the thought of forcing someone else to do these things.

I couldn't wait to tear it all down around them. To watch them all be buried in the rubble of their greed.

"Keep focused, Zack. The goal tonight is to get the girls out." Dimitri said, a firm hand on my shoulder. This was the first time in weeks that I'd seen him look human. He'd been working hard behind the scenes, trying to get my sister back. Losing himself to the chase and booze. The man really did have it bad for my sister and he would do anything to get her out tonight.

The man was fucked up without Cherry. Without his wife who no one could ever know about. Not with the shit we were into.

"I know." My eyes scanned the room. Taking in every exit we could use to slip out should shit go sideways tonight.

We would play by Dimitri's rules tonight. Damon and I were just here as the muscle. My hand itched to grab the gun hidden in the waistband on my suit tonight. Jaw working overtime on the piece of minty gum I'd thrown into my mouth before coming inside.

I needed a fix, but I wouldn't fuck up my sobriety now. It had been years of being clean and I couldn't do my job strung out.

Dimitri seemed to relax next to me, the same sign of relief coming from him as he looked at every display, searching for her in the crowd.

"Thank goodness she isn't being forced into this mess." I said, a weak smile on my face as I tried to ease my own agitation.

My eyes halted then on a curvy little redhead who was strapped to a St. Andrew's cross. Her stomach being whipped, red welts covering her pale flesh. Her aurora blue eyes were glassy and tears leaked down her freckled cheeks.

Something about her catching my attention unlike anyone ever had. Causing me to flinch with every strike to her skin.

Even as we walked towards a far wall for a better vantage point, it was as if our stares were locked. As if even in the haze, she was begging me to save her.

I barely even registered that Cherry had made it to us. Speaking in a low voice with Dimitri and Damon.

As soon as I'd embraced my sister, knowing she was okay, I was on the move. Slipping closer to the woman who had placed a hook into my heart. Drawing me to her as if I were under some sort of spell.

Finding the closest guy with a tablet, I approached, never taking my eyes off the girl.

"May I help you, sir?"

I couldn't even focus on taking him in. "I want her."

I pointed to her, my eyes taking in every inch of her perfect body.

"How long would you like her for? She's a very popular one tonight." There was a smile in his voice, causing me to finally break eye contact and take in his aging appearance. The man looked like he should be retired, not working for a fuck like Lorenzo.

"For good. She's leaving with me right now." Shock filtered across his face.

"Sir. In order to do that, you would need to pay millions…"

"I don't give a shit."

No matter what the cost. She would be mine.

Chapter Two

Zack

"What can we do for her, doc?" I asked, watching the girl sleeping in one of the hospital rooms.

I knew first hand how bad recovery could be from drugs and needed to get her the best help.

"According to the tests there was ecstasy and fentanyl in her system. We can give her some medication and supervision to help her over the next few days. But the fentanyl withdrawals could last weeks, depending on how long they had her on them." The old doctor clapped me on the shoulder, squeezing firmly. "You aren't going to want to be around for all that. But I promise she is in excellent hands."

"I'm not leaving her until I'm sure she's safe." I said, slumping down into a chair outside the door.

That girl had probably been through hell.

I wouldn't leave her alone for any of it. I'd help her just like every other person we'd saved from the bastards who'd taken them. If she had family, we'd get her to them. If not, we'd make sure she was set up with a nice life. It was the least a couple of rick pricks like me and the guys could do.

With a sigh, I rested my head back on the wall, closing my eyes as I thought over what the hell I'd just done.

I'd just bought her to give her freedom. Completely out of character for me and not how we normally did things. Damon hadn't just hired me on as a bartender, but I was the guy who helped Jensen scout out the enemy. Helped stop girls from getting too far into the system. Saving as many as we could during transition times in the underground, when they would move their stock from one place to the other.

Never before had I forked out three million just to save someone from a party, but I couldn't just leave her there. It was like my heart couldn't take the thought of leaving her to any more of what she had endured.

I wouldn't even pretend to understand what she'd been through or for how long.

All I knew was that I needed to protect her, get her better, and be whatever she needed me to be.

Chapter Three

Lily

Everything fucking hurt.

For the first time in who knows how long I could feel too much. Feel the sweat causing my hair to stick to my face. The body aches that racked through my entire body, sending shivers over me until my teeth chattered. My head felt foggy, and I had no clue where I was when I opened my eyes to bright fluorescent lights and found myself in some sort of hospital room. Or what my exhausted mind thought was a hospital. It even smelled like a hospital. The scent of cleaner, medical supplies, and death filled the space. Making my stomach churn with nausea.

I was dressed in one of those ugly paper gowns that was sticking to my skin from all the sweat. Looking around to take in the room, I found myself hooked up to an IV and a heart monitor. Taking in all the details for the first time since I'd been taken.

How long had it been?

My life had become a blur in the hands of all those assholes. I didn't know what day it was or where I even was.

The last thing that seemed clear was the night everything happened. The night my entire world turned upside down.

I was brought out of my thoughts by the sound of the door opening and a blonde guy dressed in ripped jeans and a faded band t-shirt to show off his tattooed arms, walking into the room, a bouquet of white roses and stargazer lilies held in his hand. The sight of the arrangement sending a sad pang to my heart. They had been the same thing my mom always arranged for me on birthdays and on special occasions.

"You're finally awake." He said. His voice was smooth and confident as he sat the flowers on the bedside table in a simple glass vase.

"Who are you?" My voice sounded dry and scratchy, from lack of use I supposed. I tried to clear my throat, my tongue sticking to the roof of my dry mouth.

"Oh, you have a cute little accent." The guy smiled, pouring a cup of water to hand to me. I took it gratefully, nearly chugging down the entire thing. "I'm Zack, by the way. Hope you don't mind, but we needed to know who you were, so we ran your prints and all. Turns out you've been missing for two and a half years, Lily."

I must have still been shivering, because he pulled an extra blanket from a wardrobe to drape over my shoulders before refilling my cup again.

"Two and a half years?" I asked, voice sounding weak as I stared blankly at the water sitting in my lap.

"Yeah. You were reported missing by your sister, Rose, on May 17th of 2021." He took a seat next to me. "The shivers may last a little while, along with the thirst. They had to you some strong shit. You've been going through the worst of the withdrawals for two weeks now."

"What's today?" I asked, taking a sip of the water. Still not looking at the man who seemed to know everything about me and my situation.

"November 12, 2023. As soon as you're feeling better, we can get you settled and get in contact with your sister. Our guy is on the lookout for her. Trying to find a way to get in touch."

"Who is *we?*" I asked, finally turning to face him, pulling the blanket tighter over my shoulders as I sat the cup on the bedside table next to the flowers.

Zack's hand reached to scratch the back of his head, a charming smile brightening up his face as his green eyes watched me. "Some friends of mine. Don't worry. We will do everything we can to help get you set back up and in touch with your family."

"Why should I trust y'all?" I asked, looking him over, waiting for any tell that he was lying to me.

"Damn, you talk pretty, sweetheart." His smile grew wider as he leaned forward to get closer to me, but still maintaining for distance. "You'll just have to. If not, we can't be friends, can we?"

He threw a wink in my direction. The same goofy ass smile on his face. I rolled my eyes, laying back in the bed.

Obviously, he didn't want me for the same reasons as Enzo. He'd gotten me clean and hadn't pushed himself into my personal space. I could play this by ear for a minute, especially if it meant finding my sister faster.

Fucking two and a half years. All I could do was hope that she was okay. I pulled the covers up further around my shivering shoulders, closing my eyes and praying that sleep would come to me quickly.

I just wanted to sleep until my body felt like it was mine again.

Chapter Four

Lily

The week went by in a flash. Doctors and nurses coming in to check vitals and giving me low dose medications to make the transition off all the drugs less traumatic to my system. Every day, Zack would stop by to check on me. Offering help that I wasn't willing to accept.

His people still hadn't found my sister, and it was starting to annoy me. It's not like she could just disappear into thin air.

"I need to find my sister, you fucking asshole!" I screamed. Throwing the new vase of flowers Zack had brought me at his pretty head. He ducked out of the way, the glass shattering against the hospital wall.

The more I began to feel human, the angrier I seemed to get.

The doctor said it was a side effect of the drugs that those people had me on for so long.. That in another week or two, I would begin to feel more like myself.

At least that's what they kept telling me.

The thing was, I had no clue who I was. Those assholes had taken me. Wiping away two and a half years of my life as if it meant nothing. I was finally going to have a better life for myself and my little sister. She'd been nearly eighteen when I was taken.

My thoughts raced as I tried to piece together the girl I'd known. Where would she have gone if I didn't come back? How long had she been looking for me? Had she managed to move away from that shitty little town and start a better life? Go to school? Maybe find love and begin carving out a better future for herself?

I hoped for the best. Hoping she'd had a better life than I ever could have given her. But that little voice in the back of my head told me otherwise. A sinking feeling in my gut, saying that the worst had happened, and I needed to find her.

"I promise Lily. We will find her just give us time. I'm working on setting you up at my place to make sure you're taken care of while we keep looking for Rose. We don't want those assholes coming after you again -"

"How fucking long, Zack?" I was reaching for a cup to throw at him next. My hand wrapping around the smooth ceramic.

Before I could think about actually throwing the damn thing, Zack was in front of me. Gripping my wrists in his hand, causing the cup to fall and shatter on the hard linoleum floor. My hands were pressed over my head and I'd been backed into the wall. Zack standing over me as his eyes flamed with an array of emotions.

"Calm the hell down, Lily." His breath ghosted over my face, the minty smell of his gum filling my lungs as he held me in place. "I am only trying to help you, but you have to let me."

"I don't fucking need your help." I bared my teeth at him, snapping my jaws like a vicious animal. Hoping to get him to back the hell up out of my space.

"Would you be happier if I had fucking left you there?" He was nearly yelling in my face. Hand tightening around my wrists. "You were chained up, drugged, and being fucking whipped while a room full of people watched. Watched you like some animal for their own sick entertainment. No one else would have gotten you out of there, but I did. I couldn't stand to see the tears streaming down your face." His free hand moved to brush a thumb down my cheek, stopping to tug at my lower lip. "I couldn't just leave you like that, sweetheart."

"Stop fucking calling me that." I tried to force more anger into my voice, but images from my time with those people were filtering through. Hazy. Like I was seeing them through a fogged up mirror. Like it wasn't my life at all.

Everything felt so wrong.

All the emotions I was feeling must have shown on my face, because the next thing I knew my hands were free and Zack was wrapping his arms around me. Pulling me into a tight embrace. My arms going around him to pull him closer as the tears finally fell.

What the hell had become of my life?

"It wasn't supposed to be like this," I whispered, silent tears burning my eyes as I buried my face in his chest. Soaking through his t-shirt.

"I've got you, Lily."

Chapter Five

Zack

Today seemed to be a better day for Lily as I watched her walk around the apartment. She was finally doing well enough for the doctor to allow her to be discharged and I'd ensured she'd be put with me.

The mood swings might continue, but I didn't think I'd need to worry about her falling off the wagon with her sobriety. After some conversations, it had become clear that prior to being taken this girl rarely even drank, much less did anything else. The only thing she'd enjoyed had been cigarettes, which she'd taken to smoking again when the withdrawals from the other shit got to her.

Last night's meltdown seemed to have done her some good. She seemed more relaxed, albeit suspicious of coming to stay with me.

I'd given her free rein of the apartment, but made it clear she'd need someone with her at all times until we were sure that Enzo wouldn't be sending someone to claim her again.

Angel was still with him, but my sister was free. Though Damon wasn't taking anything well. A week after the party, he'd thrown the keys to Hellfire at us and took off. The only person who knew where he was being Dimitri.

In the meantime, when I wasn't looking after Lily, I was putting a team together for an extraction mission. In just over another week, we'd have the whole gang back together.

Lily was currently making a cup of coffee in the kitchen and I couldn't help watching her. Her hips swayed rhythmically as she hummed to some song in her head while putting spoonfuls of sugar into her mug.

"Were you a dancer?" I asked, popping another peanut into my mouth.

Her head turned quickly in my direction, nearly spilling milk onto the counter she'd been about to pour into her cup.

"I thought you looked into me." She asked, turning back to her coffee. The humming and swaying sadly coming to an end.

"Just who you were. I didn't dig into work history or anything like that. I'd much rather hear all that from you." I smiled, winking at her as she made her way into the living area before taking a seat on the couch with me. Making sure to keep some distance between us.

She rolled her eyes at my flirtation, taking a long sip of her coffee.

"Yes, I was a dancer. It was the best way to give my sister a chance at a better life as a high school dropout." Her eyes stayed glued to the TV as she spoke. Hand idly stirring her coffee with a spoon.

"You dropped out of high school?" There was a lot to unpack with her statement, but that seemed like a good place to start.

"Yeah, during my senior year." Her eyes grew sad, fingers no longer stirring her coffee. "My mom died when I was seventeen. Late stage mesothelioma. She left everything to me and I dropped out to take care of my sister. Started out working as a graveyard shift cashier at the local convenience store until I realized I could make more dancing on a pole every night."

"I'm sorry about your mom." I wouldn't mention how I lost both my parents. Those assholes never meant anything to me, but from the look on Lily's face her mom had been one of the good ones.

She sniffled, tears lining her lids that she refused to let fall, taking another drink from her mug before shrugging her shoulders, "It's life."

We sat in silence for a bit, both watching the random crime show that was playing on the TV. Since getting here and giving her the remote she'd been watching crime shows. It was sort of like a documentary about serial killers and the crimes they committed that got them caught. One segment was about a string of business executives in cities along the coast ending up dead, the most recent being that of billionaire Madax Ashford.

A smile tugged on my lips as I watched. Lily must have noticed the change in my demeanor.

"What's that look for?" Her brow quirked up in curiosity as she regarded me.

"No reason. I just happen to know a lot about this one. My friends, the ones helping to look for your sister, are the sons of Ashford."

"You've got to be shitting me? Are you serious?" She was squealing, jumping closer to look at me and nearly spilling her coffee on the couch.

"Yes, now chill out before you fuck up my couch." I couldn't help the smile that tugged on my lips. Earning a light punch to the arm from the fiery redhead. "I'll introduce you to one of them tonight. He's married to my sister and the other you'll meet in about a week."

"You have a sister who is married to a billionaire!" She was very easily excited it seemed.

I couldn't help but smile at her as her eyes shone with interest. She'd be in for a real treat when she met Damon and Angel.

Chapter Six

Lily

"It's so good to finally meet you." A blonde who looked a lot like Zack pulled me into a tight embrace. Her grumpy ass shadow sitting at the bar looking annoyed dressed in a three-piece suit.

"I'm Cherry, by the way. Zack's twin sister." Her smile was bright, making her jade green eyes seem brighter in the deem lights of the club.

Apparently, Zack and his sister worked at a club called Hellfire. Which was owned by Damon Ashford. He was surprisingly absent, Zack assuring me that I'd meet him soon.

"It's nice to meet you too, Cherry." I felt awkward, but put a smile on my face as I was then introduced to Dimitri, Cherry's secret husband, and the other staff members.

Tonight, I would just be spending time at the bar while Zack was working. I was free to do as I pleased so long as I stayed inside the club.

When the place finally opened up for the night, it was a madhouse. The place was brimming with people, and I wasn't sure how Cherry and Zack managed to do it all on their own. Dimitri only lingered at the bar until his business partners showed up, moving to the upstairs VIP area. That left me at the bar, watching Zack work his magic on every pretty girl who ordered a drink. That charming smile never left his face as he worked. Tattooed forearms and hands working effortlessly to pour and serve drinks at a rate I couldn't even follow.

Even I had to admit that he was charming as hell. It must have come in handy when getting people to fork over a shit ton for the drinks he served. They were pretty basic as far as prices went for drinks in a bar, but he was making a hell of a lot in tips too.

Watching him work reminded me of when I used to dance. What took me being half-naked he did with a simple smile, a few compliments, and a well-placed wink.

I was content just to watch as I sipped my water and munched on some nachos Cherry had offered me at the start of the night. Telling me they were from her favorite food place and she'd have to take me soon. When I finished up the food and my water, I watched as Cherry made her way back to the bar, filling orders and placing them on a tray.

"Could I help?" I asked her, seeing that she was starting on a second tray.

She smiled at me. Always the happy type, no matter how busy. "Sure, if you want to. I'll have Dimitri pay you at the end of the night for your help. Usually there is another girl working, but she's..."her sentence cut off short. As if she didn't know how to finish it.

Whatever it was, I knew better than to pry. Nodding with a smile and moving to grab the second tray.

It felt nice to be useful where I could and for once I didn't have to take my clothes off to earn some decent cash.

Chapter Seven

Zack

The days just kept flashing by as me and the boys finalized all the details for the mission. Dimitri and Cherry left yesterday to go grab Damon from wherever he'd run off too. Leaving me and Lily to run Hellfire. Thankfully, it was only week nights we'd have to worry about.

We'd be closing the place this weekend to make sure everything went according to plan. With the mission taking place on Friday, we wanted to make sure we didn't have anything else to worry about. All that mattered was getting Angel out of that place and us all making it back home in one piece.

Two days from now we'd have everyone back where they belonged and Lorenzo would no longer be a problem for us. Jensen had tracked down a distant relative, Gabriele Russo, to take over the business. He'd answer to Dimitri and Damon directly and had been a big help when getting all the needed intel to make our mission a success. Gabriele was a prime example of why you didn't treat your inner circle like shit.

While we couldn't completely topple the empire of Lorenzo Russo, we could change the way things were done. Making it a legitimate business rather than some black market dealings.

Currently, I was wiping off the bar top while watching Lily speak with a few regulars. The place was dead, so we had plenty of time to just relax and have an easy night.

The DJ played random songs on his turntables for the few on the dancefloor, a small group in the back playing rounds of pool, and a few other patrons scattered around the seating areas and tables.

Lily's hips swayed as she danced from person to person. Cleaning up empties and taking orders as she went. A flirtatious smile on her full rosy lips.

The girl didn't even have to try to gain the attention of every guy in the bar. She oozed confidence and sex appeal despite all she'd been through. Other than the occasional mood swing, she seemed to be doing well with getting off the drugs, too.

She was still pissed about us not having more information on her sister, but after learning all that was going on with our little group she seemed content to be patient. Cherry assured her that as soon as we had Angel back all our resources and time would be spent finding out anything she needed.

Lily and Cherry had become fast friends after meeting. She trusted my sister a lot more than anyone else in the group. I wondered if it had anything to do with her past experiences with men or perhaps what she'd gone through after being taken, but it wasn't my place to pry.

From what little she had told me, men had always been a sore subject in her life. Her mom had been a single mom, stating that it had been a random hook up. When her mom found out she was pregnant, she had no way of finding the guy and so Lily had never known her father. Then at the strip club where she'd worked, men were selfish pigs who used her. And finally Lorenzo had kidnapped her and forced her into the skin trade.

I couldn't blame her for how she felt, either. If I had been in her situation, I would have burned the world down by now. Yet here she was with a smile on her face, as if she hadn't endured hell.

Slowly, she was beginning to trust me. Opening up and sharing parts of herself she probably hadn't shared with anyone else. But I kept my distance out of respect. Letting her hold the reins. She deserved to have all the freedom possible, and I'd give it to her.

Chapter Eight

Zack

The mission had been a shit show.

I stumbled into the apartment, kicking off my combat boots and pulling the blood stained vest from my chest. Tossing everything to the floor with an audible thud. Not giving a shit about decorum I stripped out of the dust and blood covered clothes, strolling towards the bathroom to wash the day away.

Shit had gone completely sideways.

"What the fuck, Zack?" A shocked gasp came from the spare room. I needed to get clean before talking to anyone. Not caring that I was walking through the apartment naked. Blood caked on my skin and in my hair.

46

"Give me a minute." I waved my arm, slamming the bathroom door behind me. Stepping into the shower and not giving a shit that the water ran cold as I watched the red stained stream swirl down the drain.

"Fuck," I breathed, punching at the shower tile.

It was times like these when I hated this life. Hated that I didn't have a fix. My jaw clenched tight as I tried to breathe through my nose.

With a final curse, I turned to begin washing the filth that covered me. Letting every feeling I had over what happened today flow down the drain along with the mix of water and blood.

Chapter Nine

Lily

I'd never seen anyone look the way Zack did. Pain shining in his jade eyes and worry creasing his brow. Lips set in a firm line, which was such a stark contrast to his usual carefree smiles.

He'd been covered in dust and blood. The sight doing something to my near non-existent libido. Now that I wasn't going to think too long about.

His gear was piled at the front door while he showered. The sound of curses and fists hitting tile loud even through the walls of the place.

I decided to make myself useful. Moving to clean up the gear. Taking it to the laundry room to wash.

Looking everything over it looked like everything could be washed except the bullet-proof vest. So I set that to the side and started looking through a first aid kit that was up on a shelf. Thankful when I found the small bottle of hydrogen peroxide. Beginning to apply it to all the stains before tossing it into the wash.

Next was to tackle the vest, scrubbing at the material with the peroxide as I hummed a song my mom used to sing to us when we were kids.

When I was sure the vest was as clean as it would get, I placed it to the side to dry and made my way back into the kitchen. The shower was still going, so I turned on the TV to whatever crime show was playing and made a glass of whiskey. Taking a quick shot myself, enjoying the burn of the liquid, before filling a new glass for Zack.

Something told me he needed it after the day he had.

About the time I'd placed the cap back on the bottle, Zack was coming out of the bathroom. Steam following him as he walked out in nothing but a towel slung low on his waist. My eyes trailing over his muscular form and the array of tattoos I hadn't seen before. Water running down a set of washboard abs that led to a tapered waist and that yummy V that most guys didn't have. There wasn't an ounce of fat on him and I was nearly drooling as I walked closer to hand him the glass of whiskey.

A brow raised in my direction as he took the glass before tossing it back. A sigh leaving him as he closed his eyes at the burn it must have caused with his head tilted back. The sight of his Adam's apple bobbing as he swallowed bringing a heat to my face.

"I thought you might need it." I whispered, forcing my gaze back to his face, those green eyes of his now watching my every move.

"Thanks," he said, finishing off the glass and moving to get another one. Giving me the perfect view of his towel covered ass.

I nearly forgot to breathe as I watched the corded muscles of his back flex while he poured another glass full of whiskey. The demon wings, looking almost bat like, on his back, moving with every muscle underneath the artfully designed skin.

Fuck, he was nice to look at. His blonde hair was wet and disheveled as he leaned back against the counter drinking the second glass much slower. Eyes tracking over me, causing heat to course over my skin.

"Do you want to talk about it?" I had to change the subject. Anything to get the image of him between my legs or running my tongue down his sculpted body out of my head.

He sighed at my question, eyes falling to his glass. Watching the liquid as he slowly moved the glass to swirl the whiskey within.

"Lorenzo is in the hands of our enforcer. The empire is in rubble so that we can rebuild. But -"

He seemed to struggle to finish his sentence. A need to comfort taking over as I stepped forward to stand in front of him. My hand reached without thought to touch his chest. The muscles twitching underneath my palm as I looked up into his grief-stricken face.

"Angel was shot. She's at the hospital for surgery. We don't know if she's going to make it." He seemed to not be able to take a breath as he spoke. Like the words and emotions were choking him.

"If she's even half the woman that you and Cherry say she will get through this. Until then, let's relax and hope for the best. They will call you if anything happens or they need you."

He swallowed hard, setting the half empty glass on the counter and closing his eyes. Finally, taking a deep breath as I ran my nails lightly up his chest and to his neck where the veins seemed to throb. Along his jaw and into his wet hair. The water turning the strands a darker shade of blonde than normal. I slowly stroked the soft stands, watching as his shoulders began to relax, inch by inch.

He was always an attractive guy, but it was as if I were seeing him for the first time. Seeing the side of him that very few got to see. The Zackary Vahn who was broken and yet somehow, skill a strong man who would do anything for the people he loved.

His eyes shot open moments before his lips crashed down onto mine. The kiss scorched me from the inside out and I fisted my hands in his hair. His hands gripped onto me by my waist as he pulled me flush against him. The movements causing the towel around his waist to drop and the hard length of him to press into my stomach.

Chapter Ten

Zack

Her touch sent flames through my blood as I forced my lungs to take in a breath.

Lily was right and her nails scratching lightly over my skin had allowed me to finally come to terms with everything that had happened today.

Things didn't go as planned, but Damon would move heaven and earth to make sure that Angel pulled through. That soon she'd be waking up to kick all our asses for leaving her there for so long, even though it had been her idea.

Fingers threaded through my hair, causing my tense muscles to relax as I focused on the beautiful little southern belle in my kitchen. The one who's hands touched me with such gentleness it made my heart ache. As I took in her sweet scent. A heady mix of casaba melon, freesia, and plum that had my cock instantly aching.

Fuck, I wanted her.

Wanted to touch her and feel what it would be like to sink into her warm pussy. To hear the sounds she'd make as I fucked her to the point she saw stars dancing in her vision.

I opened my eyes. Focusing in on her pink full lips. The light dusting of freckles over her pale skin. Taking in the skimpy little crop top and shorts she wore when she was lounging or getting ready for bed.

Without taking a moment to think, I swooped down, capturing her lips with my own. My hands gripped onto her curvy hips to pull her flush against me. A groan left me as my towel fell to the floor and I felt the smooth skin of her stomach against my aching cock.

I expected her to draw back and slap me. But to my surprise her hands tangled in my hair, pulling me closer as she stretched up on her tiptoes to deepen the kiss.

It was hungry. Insatiable. And I wanted more. I wanted all of her and I moved to lift her from the floor. Her legs wrapped around my waist as I turned to sit her on the kitchen counter. Putting her at the perfect height for my dick to press against her warm center. The crotch of her shorts drenched with her need and I groaned at the feeling.

Reluctantly, I broke the kiss, my lips trailing down her slender neck as I rocked against her heat. "If you want me to stop, just say the word. But until then, you're mine, sweetheart."

I bit into the tender flesh where her neck met her shoulder, sucking at the sting it caused as her legs around my hips tightened. A low groan of pleasure ghosting past her lips.

I needed to taste her. To see if she was just as sweet as she smelled. Kissing down her body as my hands worked her shorts down her thighs. Moving away just enough to unwrap her legs from me and pull the damning fabric completely off. Leaving them on the floor with that stupid fucking towel. My mouth moved to the hardened peaks of her breasts that were visible through the thin material of her shirt. Taking one between my teeth through her shirt while my hand slid up her thighs. To the junction of her shapely legs. To the place I wanted to taste. Slipping a finger through her wet folds, up to her swollen clit. Working her in slow circles until her hips were rocking against my hand. Gasps of pleasure and my name falling from her beautiful lips was music to my ears as I worked her higher and higher. Pushing a finger and then a second into her welcoming cunt. My thumb continued to work that bundle of nerves until she was gushing around my fingers. Dripping onto the counter as I sucked her other nipple into my mouth through the thin fabric of her shirt.

"Oh god, Zack," she moaned, continuing to grind against my hand as I moved to kneel on the floor, putting my mouth in line with her perfect, pink pussy.

"That's one." My voice sounded huskier as I ran my tongue against her clit. Her core was still fluttering around my fingers as I sucked it into my mouth. A gasp leaving her as she nearly bucked off the counter. But I didn't stop. Working my tongue and fingers in tandem until she was soaking my face. A groan of pleasure at the sweet nectar of her filling my mouth. And I licked and sucked until she was over-sensitized to my touch. Her hands fisting in my hair while she ground her perfect cunt against my face.

When the contractions of her muscles began to still around my fingers, I pulled them out, standing to tower over her as I brought the digits to my mouth. Sucking her remaining juices from my fingers with an animalistic groan. Her hooded eyes watched my every move as she leaned back on the counter. Spread wide for me still as she panted.

"Two," I said, moments before kissing her again. My hand fisting in her hair to pull her back to an upright position. My cock was hard as a rock at the entrance of her welcoming heat. Legs wrapping around my hips, pulling me closer as I devoured her. My tongue seeking hers in an erotic dance.

She kissed me back with just as much force as I pressed the tip inside her dripping cunt. The extra lubrication from her orgasms making it easy to slip into her tight hole. Feeling her stretch around my length as she took inch after inch.

Her groaning my name against my lips had my control slipping. I thrust completely into her in one swift movement of my hips. Burying my cock balls deep as her inner walls clamped around me.

"Fuck, you feel so good, sweetheart." I trailed kisses down her neck. Fist tightening in her hair further as my other found her hip forcing her to grind that wonderful pussy against me. Working her body moments before I pulled out only to slam back in.

She took everything I gave her. Moving her hips in time with my thrusts as we fucked each other. Riding out the pleasure until she was convulsing around my length. The tight clench forcing me to release my spend deep into her center. Moans of pleasure leaving us both as we came together. Her pussy contracting around my length. Prolonging the ecstasy that sent shivers down my spine. I wanted it to last longer. To live buried deep in her. Hearing my name praised in those breathy little moans of hers for the rest of my life.

"So fucking perfect." I whispered against her lips. The kisses turned calm and langued as we came down from the high.

"Zack.," Her voice sounded full of wonder as she kissed my lips, nails dragging down my chest, causing my cock to twitch inside of her, already growing hard again.

"Three. Next time we go for six."

Her eyes flew wide at the statement. A smirk gracing my lips before I claimed her mouth once more. If she thought I was done with her, she was in for a rude awakening.

She was the balm to my soul I'd been needing after this shit day and I wanted more.

I'd be damned if I didn't stock these fires that seemed to be burning us alive.

Chapter Eleven

Lily

I woke in an unfamiliar bed, and muscular arms wrapped around my middle. Light snores of a man sleeping causing a small smile to form on my lips as I remember everything that had happened the night before.

Turning over, I found myself looking at the most handsome man I'd ever seen. His blonde locks were a mess on his head from round after round of sex last night. Which ended with us both passing out in his bed. Completely tangled in each other.

My core ached in the most delicious way. A reminder of the nine orgasms from the night before. Zack had kept count of each and every one and he'd fucked me as if he couldn't get enough. There had been a fire building between us and I could still feel the sparks as I watched him sleep.

As a stripper who used to give favors, I was used to being left wanting. A little toy being the only thing that could ease the uncomfortable ache afterwards. The years under Lorenzo's thumb were still fuzzy, so I couldn't even be sure that sex had been good there either. I highly doubted it.

Honestly, last night had been the best sex of my life. Zack had been attentive. Finding pleasure in how many times he could make my body sing for him. For the first time, I hadn't had to think about how to please someone. I didn't have to think about anything and could just feel. Feel every touch, every brush of lips, the tangling of limbs.

I slipped from Zack's arms, needing a moment to myself. A light giggle left me as he pulled the pillow I'd been laying on into a tight embrace. His snores never stalling.

Being as quiet as possible, I moved out to the bathroom. Turning on the water to heat as I pulled a brush through my tangled hair and brushed my teeth. Eyes trailing over the hickies Zack had left in the middle of last night's fucking. I couldn't remember the last time I had a hickey. Maybe in high school with a football player who had no clue what he was doing?

My fingers lightly trailed over each mark as I took it all in. Looking at my reflection and not really knowing the girl with hollow cold eyes looking back at me. Life had been cruel, and it showed in every feature of my body. My fingers moving from the love bites to brush over the scars that marked my skin. Pale or pink lines running across my skin from whatever those assholes had done to me for those years.

The mirror began to fog, causing a sigh to leave me as I climbed into the hot stream of water. Letting it wash away every thought, every trace of the fun times.

I wouldn't let any of it break me. I was stronger than that and I refused to give any of those bastards any more power over me.

This was my life, and I'd make it a good one for as long as I could.

Chapter Twelve

Zack

My arms tightened around the pillow in my arms as I rolled over. The sound of the shower was the only sound in the entire apartment as I stretched, running my fingers through my tangled hair. A smile spread over my face as I remembered the crazy night I'd had.

The taste of her still lingering on my tongue and my cock lengthening underneath the sheets at the mere thought of her. The sounds she made when she came.

While I had obviously been attracted to Lily from the start, I hadn't expected anything to happen with her. Especially after everything she'd been through. From the shit she'd had to do after Lorenzo took her. The things she had to do to make sure that her sister was taken care of, and the loss of her mother who it was clear she cared for.

A thought racing through my brain causing me to sit upright in bed. Throwing the sheets from around my legs as I raced into the bedroom. Not caring that she probably needed a moment to herself.

"Seriously, Zack, I'm trying to shower." Her wet figure opened the curtain to glare at me as I threw a grin in her direction. Eyes trailing over the parts of her perfect body I could see.

"I think I know where we can find your sister."

Her eyes flew wide, fingers gripping the curtain until her knuckles turned white.

Chapter Thirteen

Lily

"Thanks for confirming, Jensen." Zack said, speaking into his phone as I stood in the living room, pacing in nothing but a towel.

He sat the phone down on the coffee table, leaning back on the couch, in nothing but a pair of black boxers, to look at me as I crossed my arms in irritation.

"Well?"

"It's really hard to concentrate when you're standing there in nothing but a towel, sweetheart." He flashed his usual charming grin as his eyes trailed down to my bare legs and up again. "Alright, sweetheart. Jensen says it looks like she stayed in your hometown. Started working as a shot girl at the bar after your disappearance and there are no signs that she left. It's like she's been living off the grid. No bank accounts, no expenses on record. Nothing."

"Fuck," I whisper, turning to walk to my room to get dressed. Hearing Zack's footsteps following after me as I drop the towel to the floor and pull an oversized t-shirt and black leggings from the dresser.

"We will find her. I already had Jensen send a group of guys out to the old club you worked at to see if they see her. If so, they will report back and we can think of a plan. Until we know for sure, we have to try to be as normal as possible." His arms wrapped around my waist, pulling me back flush against him. The clothes falling to the floor in a pile as lips trailed over my still damp neck and shoulder.

"Zack," I breathed, reaching back to fist my hand in his hair as I turned to capture his lips with mine.

I wasn't sure what this all was, but I needed the distraction. Needed to stop thinking about things I couldn't control right now.

He kissed me back, just as desperately. One hand sliding down my stomach to cup my sex in his large hand. Fingers slipping to delve between my folds that were steadily becoming soaked. Thumb circling my clit as he slipped two long digits inside my heat. Fucking me with his fingers until my knees wanted to give out. Tongues tangling as he added a third finger. His other hand skimmed up my body to cup my breast. Kneading the hardened bud between his fingers. The slight pain sending shock waves to my core. His hard cock fitted between my ass cheeks as he worked me into a frenzy of need. Moans left me as I climbed higher and higher towards my release.

"That's it, sweetheart. Let me feel that tight pussy squeezing my fingers as you come." He whispered against my lips, nipping at my lower lip lightly.

His words becoming the breaking point that caused my control to snap. Warmth flooding me as his fingers fucked me through the pleasure that consumed me.

Chapter Fourteen

Lily

After two weeks, the infamous Angel woke up.

Everyone was working to get her set up and comfortable in her apartment. Taking turns to make sure she had what she needed while on bed rest and recovering. The doctors saying that she had 5 more weeks of recoup time before she could get back to normal once she was finally released from the hospital.

She was beautiful and intimidating, but seemed to take to me fairly well. Since she was stuck in bed, she'd taken the time to help me look up everything we could find about my sister.

The people Zack had sent to the strip club had confirmed that my sister was now working as a dancer. The place was still run by Rodney, and Damon had taken the initiative to reach out as a prospective partner. Stating that he wanted to expand his business down the coast.

Angel had come up with the great idea to sneak us both into the club as some of Damon's favorite dancers. Saying that she'd had some previous experience dancing that seemed to surprise Damon. In the meantime, I began getting back into shape and getting an array of tattoos to cover up any scars left from my time in captivity. I needed to make sure that Rodney had no clue it was me or the whole plan could go up in smoke.

Five weeks would fly and I needed to make sure I hadn't forgotten anything from my years of dancing, too. Going directly to the closest store that sold polls and installing one in Zack's living room.

The boy had been enjoying the added benefits of it and my practice time. Making the experience more fun than I remembered it ever being. He'd insisted on going with us to the audition to meet with Rodney, too.

Wanting to keep me close and make sure that I was alright.

"So we go in, worm our way into the workings of the club and get in contact with your sister. Then we burn the place to the ground with Rodney in it." Angel said a wicked smile on her face that had me wondering if she'd actually go that far.

She slid her laptop towards me on the bed. It showed a blueprint of the club. The place having been renovated after I'd been taken, and a list of all current employees. The place had been purchased by Lorenzo three years ago, causing a memory to flash in my mind.

The well-dressed man showing up at the bar more often. Asking all the girls to dance for him privately in a back room. The feeling of his guy fucking me as he watched lazily drinking from his glass. As if he were appraising my skills.

Now things were starting to make sense.

Was that why I'd been taken? He'd thought I'd make a good edition to his collection? I needed to find out what actually happened to cause me to be the only girl to be taken. From the looks of it, no one else who'd danced with me had gone missing. Just some of the girls from my days, aging out and new girls coming in to take their place. My sister had started working there a year after I'd gone missing from the employment records. Starting out as a shot girl until transitioning to a dancing position.

That asshole Rodney had done what he'd threatened. Trapping my sister in his fucked up web once I was out of the picture.

What the hell could have happened that made Rose go work for him of all people? She'd been a smart kid. One of the brightest in her school. She was better than that run down, disgusting place.

I looked through the files before pushing the laptop back to Angel, who was tying her long black hair up into a messy bun before searching for more information.

"Why are you helping me with this, anyway?" I asked. Not meaning to be so blunt, but having no way to really voice the question. None of these people owed me anything and yet they were willing to just help me escape the life I'd been sold to, get me clean, and then help find my sister.

"I had a little sister once. I wasn't able to protect her, but your sister, I can help." She didn't bother looking up from the screen while she spoke.

"What happened to her?" A darkness seemed to settle over her features, causing her fingers to stall on the keys of the laptop and turn her attention back to me.

"Madax Ashford had her killed. So I made him pay for it. Him and every other asshole who'd hurt her." She seemed to be looking into my very soul with her cold blue eyes. Looking for something I wasn't sure she'd ever find.

She may have been looking for a reaction to the news. My brain put the pieces together until I was positive she'd been the person they'd talked about on the crime shows. The reason Madax Ashford was dead and that his killer was still on the loose. Looking her over, that sadistic gleam in her eyes confirmed that thoughts racing through my mind. This woman was not someone to be fucked with or underestimated.

"Good," was all I said before moving back to going through some files on the bed. New paperwork for me and my sister, a bank account, phones, and keys to an apartment where we could start fresh once this was all over. I'd never be able to pay them back for all this.

Our meeting with Rodney couldn't come fast enough.

Chapter Fifteen

Lily

Angel was finally recovered. Dressed in a sexy leather outfit that showed her tits and ass perfectly for the night. Mine being an emerald green lace set that I'd paired with a leather jacket and pleated mini skirt. My hair was placed in a long, rose pink wig and I hoped the cap and wig glue could keep it in place while dancing tonight.

"I can see why you were a stripper." Angel's eyes tracking over me, a smile spread over her red painted lips that sent chills down my spine and not in a good way. I was glad she was on my side. There was no way I ever wanted to be on her bad side.

"Thank y'all for helping me find my sister." I said. Looking at the faces of the group of people who'd saved me from my personal hell and helped me find my sister.

Angel, Damon, Zack and I were getting ready to go inside. Damon and Cherry were in the front seat of the limo that sat outside of Teasers. The place looked as run down as it had when I left. The neon sign blinking on and off at the side of the building as people stumbled from the door. Already drunk as hell before midnight.

"Don't thank us until this plan works and we can get her back." Zack placed a light kiss on my cheek before handing me a venetian mask. The black velvet material appearing to look like lace. The perfect match to the outfit I'd picked out tonight.

He handed another to Angel that was similar in style, with a smooth black finish and red feathers at the side.

She winked in my direction before slipping the mask over her face. They were meant to keep our identities safe and make sure that Rodney didn't have a clue who I was.

The air was cool. One of those nights after the heat from summer was turning into a cooler fall. I pulled my jacket tighter around my shoulders.

"Don't worry. We will slip in through the back. You and Angel will distract the boss while I slip out front to find your sister." Zack slipped his hand in mine, pulling me down the back alley that led towards the back door. I could just make out a woman in a sequin skirt kneeling on the asphalt with a dick in her mouth at the far end of the alley. Zack must have noticed too, because he grumbled something under his breath before ushering me through the back door of the club.

"This is where you used to work?" Angel asked, eyeing the nasty floors as we followed Damon through an array of halls.

"Sadly. It looks like we are heading to the private rooms for our meeting. Hopefully, those had been part of the renovations we saw plans for."

Only one set of doors was left open, and that's the room we followed Damon to. Rodney was already inside, a girl giving him a lap dance as he waited.

"Ah, you must be Damon." He said, shoving the girl over onto the couch giving us a full view of his large beer belly that was peaking out of his floral print button-up shirt and cargo shorts.

As we talked in Angel and I stood off to the side. Watching as the guys shook hands with the bastard and took a seat next to him.

"Rodney, I'd like to discuss the changes we spoke about on the phone. Zack here is my right-hand man, and I want to station him here with a few of my best girls. See how things work here, what needs to be changed. You understand." Damon's grin never faltered as he leaned back on the plush leather, his ankle crossed over to rest on his opposite knee.

"Of course! Your patronage of this establishment is much needed. I look forward to working with you and have already sent back the contracts, making you a partner of Teasers." His eyes trailed over to appraise us standing in the corner.

The feeling of his eyes on me made me feel like I needed a fucking shower. He had always made me sick when I worked here, but I had to sigh in relief when he didn't seem to recognize me.

"Your girls can slip out front to speak with the DJ and get to know how things work from the girls. Please join me at the bar for drinks while we talk shop."

Angel and I trailed behind as Rodney led us out into the club. Sensual music filled the space, mixing with the smells of smoke and stale beer.

With a nod from Angel, we split off from the group. Finding our way around the place to offer up dances while Damon talked business and Zack scouted for my sister.

The dull red neons being the only lighting in this hell hole aside from the spotlight shining on the stages where dancers stripped and slung around poles.

Tonight was going to be a long fucking night.

Chapter Sixteen

Zack

The mission was simple.

Find Rose in this pit of sex and bodies, plant bombs throughout the club, get everyone out, and blow this place to hell.

By the end of the night there wouldn't be a Teasers left standing.

Damon and Rodney sat at the bar. Chatting away about remodeling the entire building, making it higher end, and hiring more girls to work the new space. Using the makeover to draw in a higher paying clientele.

I excused myself from the bar and took my time walking through the space. Taking in every patron in the place and the girls who danced. Offering lap dances and pulling men towards back rooms for private sessions.

No little red head in sight.

It was possible that she was in the back room. So I made my way around the front, discreetly placing small detonators around as I made my way towards the back of the place.

As the doors to the back closed, it became silent. The music from the DJ cut off to a low thud as I walked past an array of doors that had *do not disturb signs* on the knobs. The faint sounds of skin on skin and moans of pleasure coming from behind the black painted wood.

This place made my skin crawl, and I couldn't imagine Lily working here. If this was renovated, I didn't want to know what it had been like when she'd been here.

My hand slipped behind my back to rest on the handgun I'd placed on my waistband. I refused to show up tonight without something should things go sideways.

The doors behind me opened once more, and I turned quickly to see a pink-haired woman slipping through. A smile pulled up on my lips as Lily turned to face me. She just rolled her eyes at my smile before slipping past me. I followed her back towards an open room.

It was similarly furnished to the first room we'd entered and close to the front of the club. It gave us the perfect opportunity to keep an eye out for anyone who walked by.

"Have a seat, and keep an eye on that door," Lily ordered as she walked over to a small CD player in the dark corner of the room. Music playing faintly after the click of a few buttons.

"I love it when you boss me around, sweetheart."

"And I love when you shut up." She drawled in that hot as hell southern twang, tossing another glare over her shoulder as she moved to the pole in the center of the room.

She gripped the shiny metal, doing a sensual spin around the pole where her heeled feet barely came off the floor.

"Watch the door."

My smile grew as she flowed to the beat of the music playing in the small space. Her movements were at ease as she slowly succumbed to the music.

Watching her dance was becoming a favorite pastime. Not only was she nice to look at, but to watch as the world faded away for her and she became the human embodiment of the beat was breathtaking.

She was a dancer through and through.

"It's a bit hard when I have you to look at." I teased.

"Try harder." She said before flipping up onto the poll in what she'd called a Russian layback when she'd been practicing at the apartment.

My eyes darted back and forth to watch her and the door. It really was hard to concentrate when she was so enthralling to watch and my cock strained against the denim of my jeans.

"Come here." I purred, leaning back on the couch with my arms stretched over the back.

With an effortless grace, she placed her feet back on the floor and started towards me. Her ample hips swayed to the beat as she walked. A glimmer of something shining in her hypnotizing gaze as she settled down to straddle my waist.

I could feel the heat of her delicious pussy through my jeans as she rested right where I wanted her. My aching cock fit perfectly against her.

"Someone got a bit excited." She rolled her hips to emphasize her words, forcing a groan from deep in my chest.

"Sweetheart, if you don't stop, I'm going to bend you over this couch and fuck that tight pussy until you forget your fucking name." I grabbed her hips, holding her down as I ground up against her. A breathy gasp leaving her pink lips.

I could already tell she was wet enough to soak through my jeans and it took every fiber of my being to stop myself from fucking her right here.

The sound of a door opening and a girlish giggle interrupted the moment and Lily went ridged on my lap.

"Rose," she whispered, slipping off my lap before the word had even registered.

I didn't have time to stop her as she called out to her sister and pulled her into the room, apologizing to the older man who only nodded and slipped back out to the front of the club.

Chapter Seventeen

Lily

I didn't think about what I was doing or what I was going to say as I shut the door to the room.

Turning to face my sister for the first time in years. A wave of emotions and shame for what she must have gone through as I looked over her outfit. Sheer material that left little to the imagination.

My god.

What had she had to go through to end up here? It wasn't supposed to be like this.

I pulled my mask off, showing my face as her eyes widened in shock.

"Lily? Crap. Lily, is it really you?"

Tears and a nod were all I could manage as she threw herself into my arms. Everything in my life falling back into place as we cried together. Brushing a hand over her hair in comfort.

"I'm so sorry Rose. I didn't mean for any of this to happen." I sobbed, holding her tighter.

She pulled away to look at me. Both of us taking in the faces we once knew. "What happened?"

"Rodney. He sold me off to some asshole who's had me locked up. What happened to you? Why are you here, of all places?" I had to know what happened to her. How she ended up working for that shitbag.

"When you didn't come home, I tried everything to find you. I was so worried that if I left, you'd have no way of finding me. Rodney showed up, saying you owed him money and forced me to work off whatever debt he thought you'd owed him. He wouldn't let me leave Lily. He..." Her words cut off again as she sobbed and all I could do was hold her through it.

"It's okay Rose. I promise. I'm going to get you out of here, and Rodney is going to pay for everything he did."

"Rose, my name is Zack. I'm a friend of Lily's. I'm going to need your help with something, alright?" Zack said, making his presence known as Rose and I turned to face him.

She appeared to take him in for a moment before nodding. "What do you need me to do?"

Chapter Eighteen

Lily

Rose rushed back out front to finish up her end of what we needed. She would send Rodney back to us while she, Angel, and Damon got everyone else out.

Zack stood by the door in a dark corner while I leaned against the pole, eyes focused on the door. A cloud of smoke surrounded me as I took another drag from my cigarette. A spider waiting for her prey to slip into her web.

"Ready for this, sweetheart?" Zack asked, pulling out his gun.

"As ready as I'll ever be."

It didn't take long before the doors to the back were opening and the sound of footsteps could be heard. My mask and wig now discarded to the side in wait for the man who'd made my life a living hell. I wanted him to know exactly who his judge, jury, and executioner would be.

I turned my back to the door, using a hand to lean against the pole, and continued smoking my cigarette as I heard footsteps at the door.

"Well, aren't you a pretty thing?" Rodney said. The sound of the door closing seemed to echo in the small space.

Taking a final drag, I dropped the butt fall to the floor, using the sole of my heel to stomp it into the linoleum. Exhaling the smoke that burned my lungs, I plastered a smile on my face and turned to face the man who'd ruined mine and my sister's lives.

The shock that filtered over his face was apparent as he took in who I truly was, causing my smile to broaden. He backed up a step, fully intending to make a break for it. But that was where Zack came in, his gun pressing into the back of Rodney's balding head.

"Now, I wouldn't do that if I were you." Zack said. A charming smile gracing his lips as his eyes flashed to me.

"Have a seat Rodney," I tilted my head towards a folding chair in the corner. "It's time we had ourselves a little chat."

"Come on, Lily. I was always good to you…" Rodney started to beg, but Zack pressed the gun harder into his head as he shoved the fucker towards the chair.

"The lady gave you an order. I don't think you want to find out what happens if you don't do as she says." Zack had never sounded so menacing. The fact he was doing all this for me, and for my sister, had my heart somersaulting in my chest.

Rodney did the only smart thing he could in this situation, taking a seat in the chair where Zack began to handcuff him to the bars. Hands and feet bound as his eyes blew wide in panic. Sweat formed on his brow as he attempted to reason with us.

"I'm so sorry, Lily. It wasn't nuttin' personal…"

"I'm not interested in your sorry excuse for apologies, Rodney. You sold me to that sleazebag Enzo, then blackmailed my little sister into working for you. You could have just let me leave that night. It would have been so simple," I started, walking forward while lighting another cigarette. Letting the fire burn bright as I took a long drag. "But you just had to do what you did."

I gripped him by his fat face. Forcing him to look me in the eye as I pressed the flaming end into his cheek. Screams of pain filled my ears as I put the flames out on his skin. The scent of burning flesh filling the air the more I burned him. Tears and snot trailing down his face as he screamed and begged for me to stop.

"Do you have any idea what they did to me? It's nothing compared to what I have planned for you." I sneered, tossing the ruined cigarette to the floor. His face was now a ruined mess. Burns littered his skin as he cried.

Zack had taken a step back, leaning against the wall with his arms crossed as he watched me work. Walking over to him, I smiled sweetly up at him, slipping my hand into his pocket to pull out his pocketknife. He returned my smile with that charming grin of his. Something twinkling in his eyes before I turned to walk back to the sniveling piece of shit sitting in that chair.

"Shhhhh, don't cry Rodney. It'll only hurt for a moment." I crooned, dragging the blunt end of the blade along his cheek.

"I'm sorry. I'll do anything you want." He was a blubbering mess as I dragged the blade down his neck, pressing the point just hard enough into his skin to draw blood.

"What I wanted was a new life. One without this place and where my sister could be safe." I dug the knife in deeper, blood slowly starting to run down his neck to stain the floral shirt he wore. It wasn't anything that would cause him to bleed out, but from the pain or fear he pissed himself. The smell mixed with the scents of sex from the room and burned flesh.

Suddenly, a loud blaring alarm went off and the sprinkler system cut on. Shouts could be heard on the other side of the club as the music stopped and footsteps could be heard rushing past.

"Looks like your time is up, Rodney. I really wish I could have taken my time, but then we'd risk getting caught.

I smiled down on the man who'd made so many lives a living hell as Zack slapped one of his bombs to Rodney's chest. I just hoped that he'd feel it as his body was blown to bits with the rest of this place.

He screamed louder as Zack offered his arm to me, and we walked out of that hellhole. Slipping out the back to the alley, we made our way back towards the limo. Angel was ushering Rose into the back, followed by Damon who gave us a nod as we slipped inside behind him.

The front of the club was already engulfed in flames from the small charges Zack had placed during his walk around. Nothing big enough to go boom, but that would send sparks and flames flying. The dancers and patrons were already rushing a safe distance away as Zack then handed me a small device. With a smile, I watched the bar grow further away as Dimitri drove us away.

With a last glance towards Rose, who was taking a drink of a bottled water, I looked back at the place I wanted to run from so many years ago and pressed the button.

The blast was felt as we drove away and the rest of Teasers went up in flames.

Chapter Nineteen

Zack

We made it back to the apartment late in the evening. The sun would be rising soon and shedding a whole new light on what we'd done last night. We'd driven straight to the nearest airport and headed back home on Dimitri's private jet.

Lily had explained everything to her sister, which the girl took in stride. The two were just happy to be together again. We all gave them their space to talk and catch up on everything that had happened over the past two and a half years.

Angel glanced back at the sisters, something like longing crossing over her face as she watched the two girls together.

"How ya doing, Angel?" I asked, offering her a martini.

She took the glass with a nod, never taking her eyes off the sisters. "I just wish someone had been there to help Jessica like this. I wish she could be here with us."

Damon reached over, taking her hand in his as he places a gentle kiss on her temple. In the process, pulling her closer to his side.

"Yeah. Thank you for helping her." I said, unsure what else to really say to that. Angel had to face her own demons with all that. She'd gotten her revenge and just needed to pick up whatever pieces were left. Damon seemed to be helping her the most with all that.

My phone dinged in my pocket. Pulling my attention away from everyone else as I read the message from Cherry saying that she and Dimitri had made it home safe.

"Well, we will leave you to get them settled." Damon said, clapping a hand on my shoulder.

"Thanks again," I said as he and Angel left.

Lily and I helped Rose get settled in the spare room, ensuring her that we'd have movers grab her things from her old place to be moved into their apartment next to mine within the next week or so.

We'd worry about getting them both into their new home slowly once everything calmed down.

Lily stayed in the guest room with Rose until she'd finally dozed off. Slipping into bed with me at six am. Her slender frame slipped under the sheets to press into my side, where I wrapped my arm around her to pull her closer.

"Thank you for everything," she mumbled, burying her face into my chest as she drifted off to sleep.

I watched her as she slept, the worry that had once creased her brow now smooth. For the first time since I'd met her, she slept peacefully. My heart swelled in my chest as I placed a kiss on her hair.

For this girl, I would burn the world down.

Epilogue

Lily

2 years later

My life had changed so much.

I now had a family of my own with the Hellfire crew and my sister was thriving in her new life.

She'd moved into the apartment next door to Zack a few weeks after everything had gone down, while the man of the hour had asked me to live with him.

My sister, being as love drunk and optimistic as she'd always been, had insisted that I had to, and that she was just next door if either of us needed anything.

It was impossible to argue with her. It always had been.

Now she was living on her own and had been going to therapy to deal with everything that had happened with our mom's death and my disappearance. She'd even gone to the local community college to get her degree in cosmetology. She wanted to open her own shop and the Ashford's were happy to help her with anything and everything she needed. She'd be setting up everything as soon as she had her license in a handful of months.

The bouncer of the club, Ray, had taken a liking to her immediately, and the two had been nearly inseparable. So I got to see her at night while I worked.

I'd decided to keep working at Hellfire. Helping Angel and Cherry with anything they needed. They'd welcomed me and my sister into their family with open arms and I couldn't have been more grateful.

I'd never be able to pay them back for all they'd done.

"Hey there, beautiful." Zack's arms wrapped around my waist, pulling me closer and nearly making me spill the creamer I'd been pouring into my morning coffee.

"Asshole, I'm trying to make my coffee." I seethed as he nuzzled into my neck.

"I can think of something much better than coffee at the moment." He growled, slipping a hand between my legs, stocking my clit through the thin lace of my panties.

A moan left my lips as he worked that bundle of nerves with expert fingers.

The coffee long forgotten.

The End

Acknowledgment

Dear Reader,

Thank you so much for reading and sticking with me to the end of this series.

I am so grateful to you for giving my debut book, "Angel of Blood" a chance and allowing me to turn it into the Hellfire Series. I hope that you've enjoyed these characters as much as I have.

It's bittersweet to think that the series that started my writing journey is coming to an end, but I hope that you stick around for all the other things I have planned.

It's been one hell of a ride and I'm glad I got to be on this journey with you.

Much love,

Hayley Briana

Also by Hayley Briana

The Hellfire Series

Angel of Blood

Angel in Chains

Sweetest of Fires

Hellfire

Fires of Damnation

Darkside Fairytales

Belong to Me

All Mad (coming soon)

Be My Guest (coming soon)

On the Hook (coming soon)

Haunting Series

My Dark Haunting

My Dark Terror

My Dark Dolly

My Dark Ending

Haunting

Fall Series

Fall From Grace (coming soon)

Fall to Sin (coming soon)

Love Me Series

Love Me in the Dark

Love Me in the Moonlight (coming soon)

About the Author

Hayley Briana is a small town author who currently resides in Colorado. As a mom & wife, she finds herself in need of some major self-care in the form of a good cup of coffee (or wine) and a good book. Escaping into a world of fantasy is Hayley's favorite pastime outside her day-to-day responsibilities. When she's not adulting or writing, you can most likely find her tucked away in her home library.

For more info on Hayley and what she is working on please visit HayleyBrianaWrites.com

Follow Hayley on Social

Instagram.com/hbrianawrites

TikTok.com/@beautyandthebookcase